NEAL PORTER BOOKS
HOLIDAY HOUSE / NEW YORK

Let's be bees.

Let's be fuzzy, buzzy bees and

For Rafe

Neal Porter Books
Edited by Taylor Norman

Text and illustrations copyright © 2025 by Shawn Harris
All Rights Reserved
HOLIDAY HOUSE is registered in the U.S. Patent and Trademark Office.
Printed and bound in November 2024 at C&C Offset, Shenzhen, China.
The artwork for this book was drawn with crayons.
Book design by Shawn Harris
www.holidayhouse.com
First Edition
1 3 5 7 9 10 8 6 4 2

Library of Congress Cataloging-in-Publication Data is available.

ISBN: 978-0-8234-5709-0 (hardcover)

Let's be birds.

Let's be chitty, chatty birds and

Let's be trees.

Let's be lofty, leafy trees and

Let's be snow.

And silent.

Until . . .

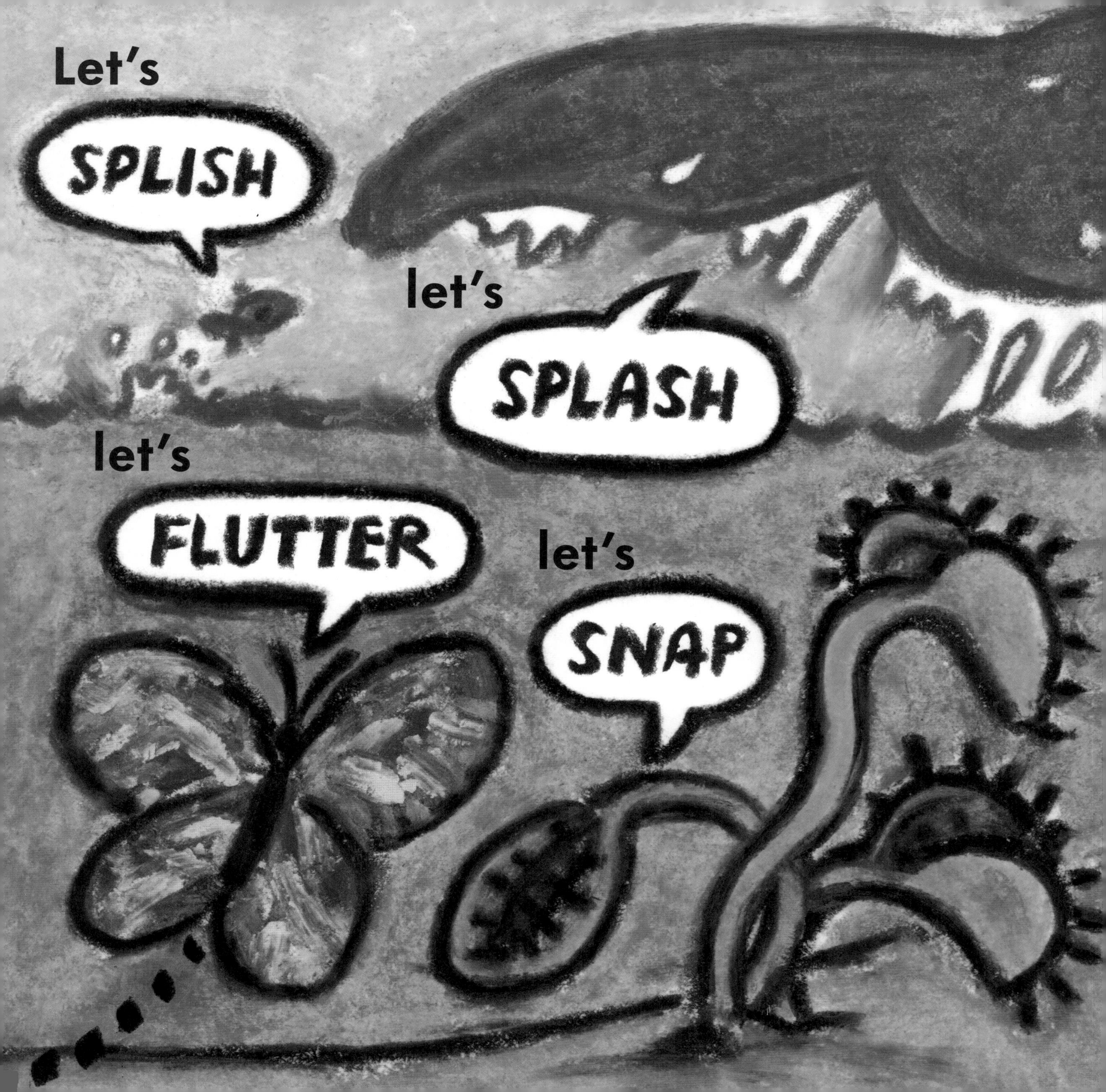

Let's
SPLISH
let's
SPLASH
let's
FLUTTER
let's
SNAP

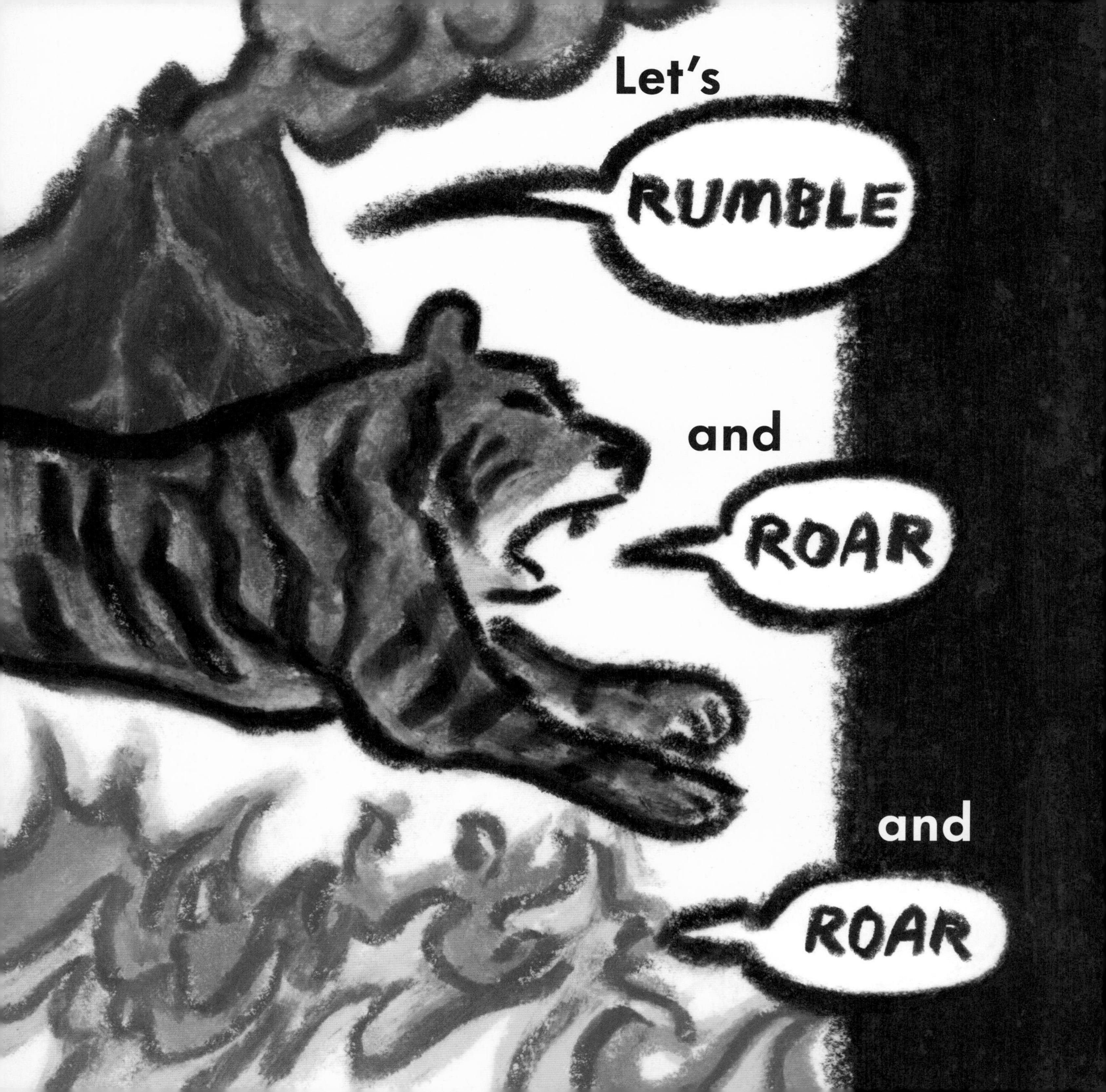
Let's
RUMBLE
and
ROAR
and
ROAR

and

and

and

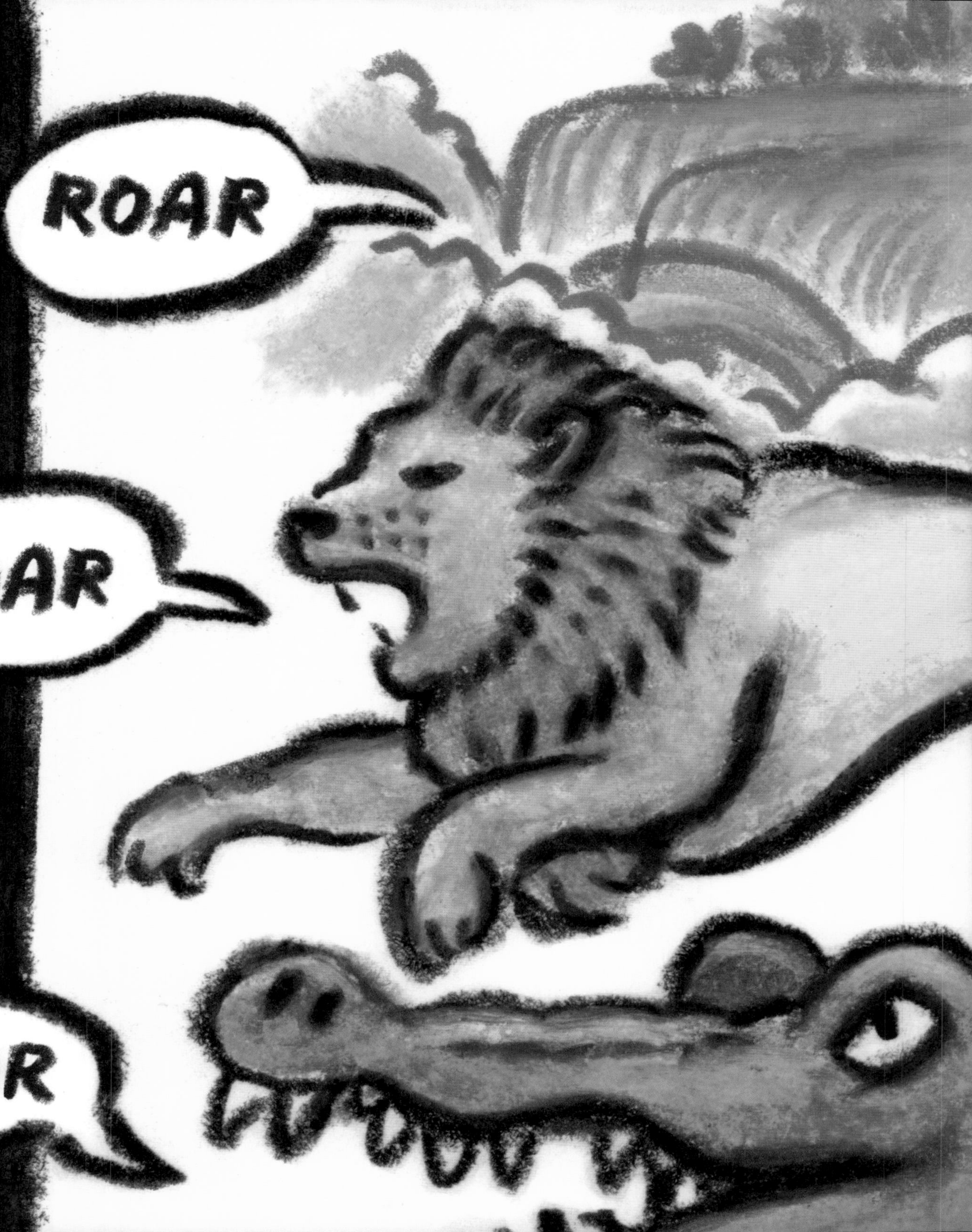

some more!

Let's make them
all at once right now!

Now let's be me and say

Now let's be you and say . . .